Magic of the Angels

DOCTOR WHO

Magic of the Angels

Jacqueline Rayner

3 5 7 9 10 8 6 4 2

Published in 2012 by BBC Books, an imprint of Ebury Publishing
A Random House Group Company

Copyright © Jacqueline Farrow 2012

Jacqueline Rayner has asserted her right to be identified as the author of this
Work in accordance with the Copyright, Designs and Patents Act 1988

Doctor Who is a BBC Wales production for BBC One.
Executive producers: Steven Moffat and Caroline Skinner

BBC, DOCTOR WHO and TARDIS (word marks, logos and devices)
are trademarks of the British Broadcasting Corporation and are used
under licence.
Weeping Angels created by Steven Moffat

The Random House Group Limited Reg. No. 954009

Addresses for companies within the Random House Group can be found at
www.randomhouse.co.uk

A CIP catalogue record for this book is available from the British Library.

ISBN 978 1 849 90286 1

The Random House Group Limited supports The Forest Stewardship Council
(FSC®), the leading international forest certification organisation. Our books
carrying the FSC label are printed on FSC® certified paper. FSC is the only forest
certification scheme endorsed by the leading environmental organisations,
including Greenpeace. Our paper procurement policy can be found at
www.randomhouse.co.uk/environment

Editorial director: Albert DePetrillo
Editorial manager: Nicholas Payne
Series Consultant: Justin Richards
Project editor: Steve Tribe
Cover design: Lee Binding © Woodlands Books Ltd, 2012
Production: Rebecca Jones

Printed and bound by CPI Group (UK) Ltd, Croydon, CR0 4YY

To buy books by your favourite authors and register for offers,
visit www.randomhouse.co.uk

Magic of the Angels

Chapter One

Amy Pond looked at the plastic bowler hat with a Union Jack pattern. 'You're not really going to wear that, are you?' she asked the Doctor.

The Doctor smiled and raised the hat politely. 'Yes. It's cool. So is my T-shirt.'

He was wearing a white T-shirt with the slogan *My companion went to London and all I got was this lousy T-shirt.*

Amy rolled her eyes. 'I can't believe you got them to print that for you!'

'At least he didn't buy the T-shirt that said *I'm with stupid!*,' said Amy's husband, Rory. 'I know he would have made me walk next to him while he was wearing it.'

'Of course I wouldn't,' said the Doctor. 'I don't think you're stupid at all. Now, come on, stupid, we're missing the tour!'

The three friends were on the upper deck of an open-top red London bus. The sun was beating down, but the Doctor still wore a tweed jacket over his T-shirt. He was sitting at the front next to the tour guide. Amy and Rory sat on the seat behind them.

The tour guide, whose name was Janet, was trying to talk about London landmarks. The Doctor was joining in, but his efforts just seemed to get on Janet's nerves.

'On your left you can see the Tower of London,' Janet began. 'Building started in the year 1066.'

'I've been locked up in there five or six times,' said the Doctor. He pointed towards the castle. 'If you squint, you can see my room. It's that window there.'

Janet's microphone picked up the Doctor's words. The other tourists laughed, but Janet ignored him.

'There's also a top secret base below the tower,' said the Doctor.

Amy tapped him on the shoulder before he could say any more. 'If it's top secret, perhaps you shouldn't mention it,' she said.

The Doctor nodded. 'Good point.' He mimed pulling a zip across his mouth.

He kept quiet until they'd crossed the river and were passing the Globe theatre. 'That's where I fought some witch monsters,' he said. 'In the old theatre, I mean, not this new one. The old one was just a little bit to the left. Of course, Shakespeare helped me fight the witches. Good old Shakespeare, he was a lovely man. His breath smelt a bit, but that's not his fault. There was no toothpaste back then.'

Everyone on the bus apart from Janet began to giggle. Amy put on large sunglasses and held her hand over her mouth. It didn't hide the fact that she was laughing.

'The London Eye was opened in the year 2000,' Janet tried a bit later. The bus was going along the South Bank.

'Oh yes,' said the Doctor. 'And then the Nestenes used it as part of their plan to conquer Earth. You must remember that. There were shop-window dummies coming to life.'

It was when the Doctor told the tourists about a pig flying a spaceship into Big Ben that Janet snapped.

The bus stopped. The other tourists booed as the Doctor was led off by the driver. Amy and Rory followed. Amy was laughing, but Rory was holding up a hand to hide his face. 'I've never been thrown off a bus before,' he said.

The Doctor looked puzzled. 'I was only trying to make things a bit more fun.'

Amy tucked her hand through the Doctor's

arm and led him towards an ice-cream van. 'Never mind. We can still do the tourist thing like you wanted. We'll just have to walk instead.'

They sat on the bank of the river eating ice-cream cones. Boats sailed along the water in front of them. Children laughed and couples held hands. 'Mmm,' said Amy, licking a blob of melting ice cream off the side of her cornet. 'This is perfect.'

'Better than fighting monsters,' Rory added as he ate the last bite of ice cream. Then he frowned as he spotted a poster on a wall nearby. 'But it's not quite perfect.'

The Doctor and Amy turned round to see what he was looking at.

'MISSING since May the sixth. Katie Henley.'

The photo showed a pretty blonde girl. She didn't seem much younger than Amy.

It wasn't the first 'MISSING' poster they'd seen that day. Most of them also showed young men or women, boys or girls.

The Doctor walked over and put up a hand to touch the face in the picture. 'So much sadness,' he said softly. 'The sadness that made her leave home. The sadness of those left behind.'

Amy joined him. She reached out her hand to touch his. 'We can't solve every problem,' she said gently.

'We should be able to!' The Doctor sounded fierce. 'What's the point of doing what we do if we can't help everyone?'

'I used to think that too, sometimes,' said Rory. 'I used to wonder why I became a nurse. There were so many people I just couldn't help. In the end I had to accept that helping some people was better than helping no one.'

'Wise old Rory,' said Amy, smiling. She linked an arm through his. 'My boys. My boys who help people.' She linked her other arm through the Doctor's. 'Come on. We're on holiday, remember.' The three of them walked off arm in arm. 'What do you want to do now?' she asked the Doctor. 'We've been to St Paul's...'

'And we got thrown out of the Whispering Gallery for shouting,' said Rory.

'They wouldn't let us in to Buckingham Palace to have tea with the Queen,' said Amy.

The Doctor frowned and pulled a crumpled paper bag out of his jacket pocket. 'I'd even brought doughnuts!' he said. 'Her Majesty loves doughnuts.'

'We were thrown out of Madame Tussaud's

when the Doctor drew on the waxwork of Guy Fawkes,' said Rory.

'Well, they'd got his moustache wrong,' said the Doctor. 'Guy was very proud of his moustache.'

'Now we've been chucked off the open-top bus tour,' said Amy. 'There can't be many more things to be thrown out of.'

They were walking along the river as they talked. The Doctor absent-mindedly took a doughnut out of the paper bag and bit into it. Jam squirted all down his chin.

Rory spotted another poster. This one did not show a missing girl. It was an advert for a show. 'We've not got thrown out of a theatre yet,' he pointed out.

'Great idea!' cried the Doctor. 'I love a show.' He looked at the poster too. 'Sammy Star, Master of Magic. Lovely!'

'Sammy Star? He sounds like he should be doing children's parties, not West End shows,' Amy said.

'Nonsense, it'll be great,' the Doctor told her. 'I love a good magic trick.' He wiped his chin with a hankie, looking puzzled. 'In fact, I seem to have made jam magically appear on my face.'

Rory and Amy looked at each other and

laughed. Still with a puzzled frown on his face, the Doctor took another doughnut out of the bag and started to eat it. Rory and Amy laughed even more.

They crossed the river and wandered through the streets. Rory and Amy both spotted several more 'MISSING' notices. Neither of them pointed out the posters to the Doctor.

They came to Trafalgar Square, and stopped to look at Nelson's Column. The Doctor patted the head of one of the huge bronze lions guarding the base. He pointed out the statues that stood on plinths at three corners of the square. The fourth corner also had a plinth, but it was empty. 'They didn't have enough money for the last statue,' he told Amy and Rory.

'I'd heard they were showing works of art on it instead,' said Amy. 'Something new every year or two.'

The Doctor nodded. 'That's right. I think they're now looking for something that can stay on it for good.' He bit into his third doughnut. 'Right. Let's see about getting tickets for the Sammy Star show!'

Chapter Two

They were sitting in the front row of the stalls. Any minute now, the lights would go out and the show would begin.

Amy flicked through a programme. 'Hey, it says here Sammy Star used to do children's parties,' she told the others. 'I know I said he sounded like he did, but that's weird. He must be pretty good to go from that to the West End.'

'He was on one of those TV talent contests,' Rory told her. 'It said so on the poster. *Britain's Got Magic*, something like that.'

'Oh yeah.' Amy turned a page. 'Got all about it here. Hang on, though, he didn't win it. "He was laughed off the programme," it says, "but he had the last laugh. Sammy Star now has a sell-out West End show. He has won great acclaim for the Graveyard Ghosts trick that forms the finale of his act." Wow. The boy's done good.'

Rory frowned. 'If this show is a sell-out, how come we got the best seats in the house?'

The Doctor looked slightly sheepish. 'Oh, I booked our tickets weeks ago. At least, that's what they told me at the box office just now. So I'd better make sure I do it. Remind me to pop back in time and buy them later, will you? The universe might collapse if I don't.' As if to distract them, he quickly added, 'Anyone like a doughnut?' He put his hand in his pocket and found only an empty paper bag. 'Someone's nicked my doughnuts!'

Amy leant across and wiped a splodge of jam off his face. 'You already ate them, you doughnut!'

The theatre was almost full now. The only empty seats were in the row behind the Doctor, Rory and Amy.

'That's odd,' said the Doctor. He looked over his shoulder at the empty row. 'If they booked seats that good you'd think they'd be keen to see the show. Yet they haven't even turned up.'

'Ooh, this might be them,' said Amy, also looking behind them. A party of elderly people was coming down the aisle. They were led by a middle-aged woman in a navy blue blazer with gold buttons. She ushered her group into the empty row, telling them to 'Hurry up! Hurry up!' much too loudly.

Just as the last of the party sat down, the lights went out. Amy heard someone behind her draw in their breath sharply.

'Don't worry, Mrs Hooper, it's just the show starting,' said a cheerful voice.

Amy thought the voice belonged to the blazer woman. She wondered why so many people thought being old was the same as being stupid.

The curtain was raised. A spotlight shone onto the stage. A figure stood in the middle of it, head bowed. It wore a black top hat and was wrapped in a cloak.

There was a rumble of drums. A voice from above said, 'Ladies and Gentlemen, please welcome Mr Sammy Star!' The drums crashed more loudly and another, brighter, spotlight followed a man swinging down from above. As he reached the cloaked figure, the swinging man kicked out. The cloak crumpled into a heap and the audience gasped.

The top hat rolled away as Sammy Star landed on the stage. He scooped up the hat and pulled a large white rabbit out of it. Then he placed the hat on his head.

Everyone clapped as he took a bow.

'Very nice,' said the Doctor, raising his voice so Amy could hear him over the applause. 'Of course, he had a second hat with a rabbit in it waiting ready for him. That's why the stage was only lit by spotlights, so we wouldn't spot the hats being swapped.'

Amy glared at him. 'Don't spoil it!' she hissed.

Amy could have saved her breath. For each of Sammy Star's tricks, the Doctor announced how it was done. He wasn't trying to show off, Amy knew that. Working out the tricks was just the bit of the show he enjoyed the most.

It was a shame Sammy Star didn't seem to enjoy it as much. At first he was clearly trying to ignore the Doctor. Later he started to twitch and glare at the front row. Amy was quite relieved when it came to the interval.

'Having fun?' she asked the Doctor as they sat in their seats at the front.

He nodded happily. 'Oh yes. Although...' A frown crossed his face and he stood up. 'Back in a minute. I just want to check out a few things.'

Amy and Rory sat for a few moments just holding hands. 'You don't think something's wrong, do you?' Amy said after a while.

'Nah,' said Rory, although he looked worried. 'Just because we've never had a holiday without monsters or crashing spaceships before...'

'Well, no monsters so far, and we've been here almost a day!' said Amy.

'Monster!' The shaky voice came from the row behind. It was a word that Amy and Rory couldn't ignore. They both spun round.

The speaker was a member of the elderly party. She looked to be in her eighties, and tears were trickling down her cheeks.

Amy knelt up on her seat and reached over the back to hold the old lady's hand. 'Hey, don't cry,' she said gently. 'What's the matter?'

'Monster,' the woman repeated through her sobs.

'Lost,' said the elderly lady in the next seat. Amy turned her gaze on her. She was also crying. 'So very lost. So lost we were never found.'

The woman in the blazer stood up. 'Just ignore them,' she said to Amy. 'Mrs Hooper! Mrs Collins! Be quiet now! You're getting on this nice young girl's nerves.'

'Oh no,' Amy replied. '*They're* not getting on my nerves.' She didn't like to hear people being spoken to so rudely, when they'd done nothing to deserve it.

'Well, you're very kind to say so,' the woman said. 'She's very kind to say you're not annoying her!' she told the two old ladies loudly. 'They were so keen to come,' she went on, turning back to Amy. 'The second they saw the poster it's been Sammy Star, Sammy Star, day and night. Now then, Miss Leake, I said to myself, here's an idea! Wouldn't it be a lovely treat, taking them to see his show! But they've done nothing except make a fuss since we got here. Monsters indeed. Why, they don't know the meaning of the word!'

'Did you live through the war, Mrs Collins?' Rory asked softly.

'VE Day...' she whispered back.

He nodded. 'She might have a better idea of monsters than you think, then,' he told the woman in the blazer, Miss Leake.

'Everyone all right?' asked the Doctor as he returned.

'I'm a bit worried, Doctor,' Amy began, but Miss Leake interrupted her.

'Nothing to worry about at all!' she said. 'We were just being silly, weren't we, Mrs Collins and Mrs Hooper?'

'Well, you might have been being silly, I'm not so sure about them,' muttered Amy under her breath.

The theatre lights dimmed again. The Doctor made his way back to his seat. Amy still felt concerned about the two old ladies, but wasn't sure what to do. She decided she would tell the Doctor all about it after the show.

The curtain rose for the second half. The Doctor didn't talk over the magic this time. He seemed troubled.

Finally it was time for the big showpiece, Graveyard Ghosts. Mist swirled across the stage, which was now covered with gravestones and statues. Amy shivered to see one that looked like a stone angel. 'Makes me think of *you know what*,' she said to the Doctor under her breath.

Tall trees twisted at the sides of the stage. A girl poked her head out from behind a tree, then crept out to the middle of the stage. She was young and pretty and dressed in a Victorian-style white nightgown. Long, dark hair curled down her back. Suddenly a pale, bony hand thrust through the turf of a grave.

In the second row of the stalls, Mrs Collins and Mrs Hooper screamed and screamed and screamed.

Chapter Three

The old ladies wouldn't stop screaming. The show kept going, but there were nervous looks from the people on stage.

Miss Leake was trying to get the two screaming women to be quiet. Rory went to join her, and helped lead Mrs Collins and Mrs Hooper up the centre aisle. Amy was going to help, but noticed that the Doctor was sitting still. His eyes hadn't left the stage.

'Shouldn't we see what's wrong?' she asked.

He shook his head, although his eyes didn't move. 'Rory will cope. Rory will be perfect. I need to see this show. I need to see it right to the end.'

Amy was torn. Go with Rory or stay with the Doctor? She dithered for a second, then sat back down. The Doctor was right. Rory would be fine on his own. He was great with old people. It sounded like the real action would be here.

On stage, Sammy Star emerged from his

grave, dressed as a skeletal monster. The mist cleared. The Doctor and Amy watched as the monster crept up behind the young girl.

She shrieked and tried to run, but sharp spikes shot through the stage floor in front of her. She backed away, but spikes sprang up behind. The 'monster' began to pluck apples from a twisted tree and throw them. They stuck, proving the sharpness of the spikes.

More and more spikes herded the girl towards the base of the tallest tree. She began to climb. The bark of the tree fell away, revealing a spiral walkway. Sammy Star scooped up an armful of daggers and moved underneath.

The girl was running now. Sammy Star thrust his daggers up through the walkway, each just missing the girl's feet. Following her, behind and below, he rammed home dagger after dagger. The blades stuck there, pointing upwards, a dangerous, glittering path.

The girl reached the top of the walkway. There seemed to be no escape for her. Sammy Star was still climbing up behind, weaving his way through the dagger points. Below, the spikes gleamed.

Finally the girl could go no further. She turned round and there was the monster, facing her. He held up a hand and opened it to reveal an apple. The girl tried backing away, but there was nowhere to go. Sammy Star threw the apple...

The apple hit the girl. With a scream she toppled backwards, falling towards the spikes.

Amy gasped. Everyone in the audience gasped, except the Doctor.

The very instant the girl began to fall, there came a blinding flash of light from the stage.

Amy blinked her eyes. When her vision cleared, she could see that the girl had gone. In the centre of the spiral, amid the spikes, stood the angel statue.

The crowd began to applaud loudly. There were even some cheers and whistles.

Amy didn't clap or cheer. Neither did the Doctor.

'The angel moved...' Amy whispered.

'Oh yes,' replied the Doctor grimly. 'The angel moved.'

'So it's...'

'It's a Weeping Angel,' said the Doctor. 'A stone-cold killer. A lonely assassin.'

As the applause died away, the lights on the stage faded. There was only one spotlight, and it was on the Weeping Angel.

'We have to keep looking at it...' said Amy

under her breath, scared. 'If we stop looking at it, it'll move. It'll get more people.'

The curtain fell.

Amy jumped up, thankful she was in the front row. She ran to the stage and clambered onto it. The audience murmured, wondering if this was part of the act. She scrambled under the curtain.

Two men were carrying the Angel off stage. 'Hey!' Amy called after them.

'Who are you?' said a voice. Amy spun around. Sammy Star had come back onto the stage. He was no longer in his graveyard outfit and was now wearing a purple suit. 'Look, I'll sign your programme if you wait at the stage door, but get out of here now, OK? Time for me to take a bow.'

'I'm not a fan!' Amy told him. 'I'm trying to save people's lives! Do you know what that statue is?'

The Doctor pushed through the curtain. 'Oh, I'm quite sure he doesn't,' he said. 'He only knows what it can do. He's just using it.'

Sammy Star stared at them for a moment. The look on his face scared Amy, it was so fierce.

'No one is going to ruin this for me,' he snarled. 'No one. Do you hear me? This is my moment.' He turned to the side of the stage and beckoned. Two burly men appeared. 'Throw them out!' he hissed. 'Make sure they don't set foot in this theatre again.'

'Time to go!' said the Doctor. He took Amy by the hand and pulled her to the edge of the stage. They ducked under the curtain, jumped down and ran up the centre aisle. The security men were close behind them.

As the audience began to applaud Sammy Star's curtain call, the Doctor and Amy made it to the exit. They raced through the foyer, nearly knocking over a lady selling *It's Magic!* T-shirts. 'Oooh,' said the Doctor, pausing for a second.

'You don't need another T-shirt!' Amy yelled, dragging him to the doors.

The security men didn't chase them once they were out of the theatre. They just stood in the doorway looking fierce.

'Yeah, and stay out!' the Doctor shouted at them, waving his fist in the air. 'Oh, hang on, might not have got that *quite* right...'

The summer sun was low in the sky now. Amy and the Doctor walked to Trafalgar Square and sat at the base of Nelson's Column.

'Weeping Angels can send people back in time,' Amy said to the Doctor. 'So when the falling girl vanished, she must have been zapped into the past.'

The Doctor nodded. 'Oh yes, it's all been very carefully planned. A Weeping Angel can't move if anyone's looking at it. The audience can see it the whole time. Even if they're not looking straight at it, it's in everyone's field of vision. In the corner of their eye. Until the very end. The light flashing so brightly dazzles them all. The Angel is free and can move. The nearest target is the falling girl. It touches her and sends her into the past. Yum yum, nice bit of time energy for the Angel, and a nice trick for Sammy Star. All the people applaud.'

'There's one thing I don't get, though,' said Amy. 'How does he bring her back? How does he do the trick night after night?'

The Doctor didn't answer. He got up and walked over to a lamp post. A poster had been stuck to the black metal and he pulled it off. He came back and handed it to Amy without a word.

'HAVE YOU SEEN THIS GIRL?' she read. 'Kylie Duncan, nineteen. Long dark hair and green eyes. Last seen wearing blue jeans and a red T-shirt.' She looked up at the Doctor, puzzled.

'Have you seen this girl?' he echoed. 'Last

seen wearing a long white nightie.'

Amy's mouth fell open as she stared at the photo on the poster. 'That's her! That's the girl we've just seen vanish!'

'People are worried,' said the Doctor. 'Worried enough to report her missing. I expect Kylie Duncan's mum is crying herself to sleep every night. She doesn't know she'll never see her little girl again. No one from this time will ever see her again.'

He jumped up and began to walk around the edge of the square. There were posters every few metres. 'Molly Crane. Brittany Hughes. Amber Reynolds. Lauren Peters,' he read as he ripped them all down. 'Each of these girls has a mum waiting at home. None of those mums will ever see their daughters again.' Amy had rarely heard him sound so angry. 'Sammy Star doesn't bring his assistants back from the past. He doesn't have to. There are hundreds of girls out here, friendless and helpless. They come to London looking for a new start. Of course they'll jump at the chance to get into showbiz!'

'Oh no,' whispered Amy. 'You mean... it's a new girl every night? Every show someone else gets sent back in time? But it's sold out for months and months!'

'Then the theatre will have to give everyone their money back,' said the Doctor grimly. 'Tonight was Sammy Star's last show. His last show ever.'

Chapter Four

Rory helped walk Mrs Collins and Mrs Hooper back to their minibus. He had an arm round Mrs Collins and could feel her shaking. Miss Leake was leading Mrs Hooper.

Miss Leake was in charge of Golden Years Home for the Elderly. She told Rory this, and a lot of other things that didn't interest him, as they walked to the car park. She also kept being cheerful at the old ladies. 'Now, don't let's be sillies!' she said. 'It was just a silly old magic trick, nothing to be scared of. Fancy being scared of ghosties and ghoulies at your age, Mrs Collins and Mrs Hooper!'

'Monster...' muttered Mrs Hooper.

'It wasn't a real monster, it was just a young lad. Like this lad here!' Miss Leake said, waving a hand at Rory. 'You're not scared of him, now, are you?'

Rory thought that Sammy Star must be at least fifteen years older than him. He didn't mention it, though. It was hard to get a word in edgeways when Miss Leake was talking.

'Lost,' said Mrs Collins. 'So lost.'

'You're not lost, Mrs Collins! We're in London – LONDON,' said Miss Leake loudly. 'Now you just need to get on the bus and we'll take you home. I said, we'll take you BACK HOME. Back to lovely Golden Years for a cup of cocoa then beddy-byes.'

Miss Leake unlocked the minibus and Rory helped the two ladies up the steps. 'Now I'm going to ask this young man to be very kind,' said Miss Leake to her charges. 'I'm going to ask him to stay here with you while I go back for the others. I hope they've not got up to mischief while I've been gone!'

She turned to Rory and gave him a would-be winning smile. 'Now, you don't mind waiting, do you? I won't be long. I can't leave my girls alone, though!'

Rory nodded. 'That's fine.'

'There, do you hear that? He says it's fine. It's FINE. You don't have to worry, because he's a nurse,' Miss Leake said, with a little giggle in her voice. 'Oh, they love a male nurse, do my old dears! Maybe you should be the one to worry!'

Rory forced a smile onto his face. 'I'm sure we'll be OK.'

Miss Leake went off, still giggling a little

to herself. Rory shut the door of the minibus, and sat down on a seat. Mrs Collins and Mrs Hooper were in the seat behind, and he swivelled round to talk to them. 'Are you all right?' he asked.

They nodded slowly. The tears had stopped falling now, but both old ladies still looked sad. They had a haunted look, Rory thought, as if they were thinking of a past tragedy.

They all sat in silence for a while. The two women were holding hands tightly, clinging to each other for comfort.

'What was it, Mrs Collins?' Rory asked softly after a while. 'What's the matter? What scared you?'

'Kylie,' she said.

Rory just gazed at her in surprise. It seemed a very odd thing to be scared of.

'Kylie,' she repeated. 'My name. Call me Kylie. Not Mrs Collins.'

'Amber,' said Mrs Hooper. 'I'm Amber. I'm not mad.'

'Of course you're not,' said Rory. 'Who says you are?'

'We have to be careful,' said Mrs Hooper. She didn't seem to be talking to Rory, her eyes were looking far away. 'We mustn't tell the truth. They'll think we're mad.'

'We'll get locked up if we tell the truth,' added Mrs Collins.

'Is something bad going on?' Rory asked, worried now. 'Is something bad going on at the Golden Years home?'

To his relief, Mrs Hooper shook her head. 'Not there,' she said. 'A long time ago. A very long time ago.'

Mrs Collins nodded fiercely. 'A very long time ago,' she agreed. 'Today. A very long time ago today.'

Rory had thought he was getting somewhere, but that answer made no sense at all.

'It was VE Day,' said Mrs Hooper. 'Victory in Europe. I didn't know what that meant, then. We didn't do it at school.'

'They asked me why I was in my nightie,' said Mrs Collins. 'Why I was walking around in a daze.'

Mrs Hooper almost smiled. 'I was dazed too. They said there was a girl like me, a girl who was confused. They wondered if we knew each other. That's how we met. We've stuck together ever since.' She squeezed her friend's hand.

'They said it must have been a bomb,' said Mrs Collins. 'A bomb must have come down and hurt our heads. That's why we didn't know what had happened.'

Mrs Hooper nodded. 'They said they'd thought the last Doodlebug had fallen months ago. People were upset to think there'd been more bombs. They said it would be the last one, though. There was peace in Europe at last. We knew it wasn't a bomb, but we didn't know what had really happened. So we went along with it.' She paused. 'We knew there must have been other girls, but we didn't look for them. It's not the sort of thing you can ask people.'

'They made us join their party,' said Mrs Collins. 'It was the biggest party I'd ever seen. Right there in Trafalgar Square. They were all so happy. We danced and danced and danced. We were so scared and so lost, but we danced.'

'I danced with a soldier,' said Mrs Hooper. 'His name was Albert. It was a summer's day like this when we got married...' Tears began to fall from her eyes again, and she began to sing. *'It may be an hour, it may be a week...'*

Mrs Collins lifted her voice and joined in. *'It may be fifty years...'*

Rory felt tears pricking at his eyes too. The two old ladies were so sad, yet so dignified.

The moment was broken. The door to the

minibus clunked open, and Miss Leake began helping elderly people up the steps. 'Everything all right?' she called to Rory, but didn't wait for an answer. 'I'm sure you've been fine, even with that cheeky pair! Mrs Collins and Mrs Hooper are so naughty sometimes. They do play such jokes. Why, the other day they tried to tell me they were born in 1993! *1893* more like, I said, didn't I, Mrs Hooper? But you will have your little joke.' She didn't seem to care or even notice that Mrs Hooper ignored her.

When the old people were seated, Rory got up and walked down the bus to the door. 'Bye then,' he said to Miss Leake.

'Goodbye, and thank you so much,' she replied, sitting herself down in the driver's seat. 'Oh! By the way! You know those friends you were with? That nice red-haired girl and the young man in the plastic bowler hat?' Rory nodded. 'Well, they got thrown out of the theatre! Awful, isn't it? So I wouldn't go back there looking for them if I were you.'

Rory sighed and shut the bus door behind him. Amy and the Doctor had been thrown out of yet another place. Lucky he still had his mobile phone. He kept it with him out of habit. At least in England around his own time it should work.

As he moved away from the minibus, he could hear the whole busload of elderly people joining in the song. *'It may be an hour, it may be a week, it may be fifty years. But I know we will find loving hearts still entwined, on the day we meet again.'*

The wartime song always made him think of Amy. He'd waited nearly 2,000 years for her. Fifty years was nothing compared to that. The song told the truth, though. Even after all that time, their love had still been strong.

Rory smiled.

Chapter Five

They met in Trafalgar Square.

'There was a VE Day party here,' Rory told the Doctor and Amy as he sat down beside them. He was still thinking of the two old ladies, Mrs Collins and Mrs Hooper.

The Doctor nodded. 'Eighth of May, 1945. Thousands gathered here. Churchill made a speech and they played it over loudspeakers.'

'Good old Winston,' said Amy. 'What?' she cried as Rory gave her a look. 'I can namedrop too! It's not just the Doctor who's been everywhere and met everyone.'

'I wasn't at the VE Day party,' the Doctor pointed out. 'I just heard about it from other people.' He sighed. 'One happy day. One great big happy day for them all. Then real life got them again. Japan was still fighting the war. Everyone had lost loved ones. Homes had been bombed. There were no bananas.'

'They were there,' said Rory. 'Those two old ladies. They were at the Trafalgar Square party on VE Day. Strange to think of it, really. More than sixty-five years ago. They'd just have been teenagers, and they were dancing right here. Maybe on this very spot.' He smiled. 'Poor old dears. I couldn't really follow what they were saying. I tell you what was weird, though. They were called Kylie and Amber. You don't think of old people being called Kylie or Amber, do you?'

'Hang on,' said Amy, looking shocked. 'Doctor...'

The Doctor stiffened. For a moment he didn't say a word, then started leafing through the pile of posters beside him. He picked out the one he had shown Amy earlier, and another of a blonde girl. He held them up so Rory could see them.

MISSING: KYLIE DUNCAN. MISSING: AMBER REYNOLDS.

Rory frowned. He took the poster of Amber Reynolds and stared at it. 'I don't understand...'

'That's because you missed the end of the show,' said Amy. 'We've got a lot to tell you. Sammy Star is using a Weeping Angel in his act. It's sending girls back into the past.'

'I think you've just found out where in the past they're ending up,' the Doctor told Rory. 'One minute they're in a West End theatre in the twenty-first century…'

'… and the next they're in 1945. At a party in Trafalgar Square,' finished Rory. 'Oh no.' He jumped up. 'We've got to go and rescue them! We know where they are and when they are, so we can go in the TARDIS!'

The Doctor shook his head. 'We also know they stay there, in that time. They grow old.'

'We could get them back to their own time!' Rory cried.

'They get back to their own time,' said the Doctor. 'They just take the long route. It takes them about sixty-seven years.' He shook his head again. 'I'm sorry, Rory. We can't change that.' He stood up. 'But we can make sure it doesn't happen to anyone else. Come on, Ponds, we're going back to the theatre. We've got less than twenty-four hours to stop Sammy Star.'

*

The sign above the theatre was still lit up. The words *Sammy Star's Magic Show!* shone out.

'The city never sleeps!' the Doctor said. He rattled the theatre doors. They were locked. 'It seems the people who work here do sleep, though. Never mind.' He pulled the sonic screwdriver out of his pocket. 'I have a key.'

The foyer looked haunted in the gloom,

more haunted than the stage graveyard. They crept across it in silence and went through a door marked NO ENTRANCE.

'I know the way,' the Doctor whispered. 'I went for a snoop around during the interval. I had a feeling something was wrong. My seventh sense.'

'Don't you mean sixth sense?' asked Rory.

'No,' said the Doctor. 'I already have six well-used senses. This was my just as well-used but often ignored Finding Evil sense. Of course all my senses are finely honed – *ooof*.'

He broke off as he walked straight into a large security guard.

'What are you doing here?' growled the guard.

The Doctor fumbled in his pocket and brought out his psychic paper. 'I've come to inspect the magic,' he said, holding out the open wallet. The guard peered at the blank paper, seeing only what the Doctor wanted him to see.

'Says here you're with the Magic Oval,' he said.

'Ah yes,' said the Doctor as he brushed himself down. 'It's like the Magic Circle, only... stretched. We inspect tricks at night so no one else finds out how they're done. If you could just escort us to Sammy Star's prop store, we'll get on with our checks.'

He made to walk past the guard, but the burly man put out an arm to stop him. 'Does Mr Star know about this? He never said you were coming.'

The Doctor tutted. 'Well, of *course* he doesn't know. It wouldn't be a random secret magic check at night if he *knew* about it. You've heard of secret shoppers? They buy things in shops and then report back on the service.'

The guard nodded his head.

'Well, we're secret magic-checkers. We check the tricks then report back to the Magic Oval.'

Amy held her breath. For a moment it looked like the guard might let them through.

'Well...' he said. Then he paused. 'Hey, haven't I seen you before?'

The Doctor looked puzzled. 'I don't think so. I've just got one of those faces.'

'Yes I have!' The man frowned. 'I threw you out of here an hour ago. I noticed your plastic bowler hat at the time.'

'Lots of people wear these!' the Doctor said. 'They're cool.'

'No they don't,' muttered Amy under her breath. 'And no they're not.'

'Yeah, but I also noticed your funny T-shirt and that you had a red-headed girl with you,' said the man. 'Come on, you're not fooling me. You're trying to nick something so you can cheat in the contest tomorrow. Well, you're out of luck. Out you go!'

*

'And stay out!' the Doctor yelled as he landed on the pavement for the second time that evening.

'I already have "theatre" on my list of places we've been thrown out of,' Amy complained. 'We could at least have found somewhere new.'

'Well, look on the bright side,' said the Doctor. 'At least we were thrown out before we got to the guard dogs. They looked fierce.'

Amy blinked. 'There were guard dogs?'

'Just a couple. I saw them when I was scouting around during the interval. Oh, and a lot of padlocks. Sammy Star really doesn't want people going through his props.'

'So what do we do now?' asked Rory.

The Doctor didn't answer at once. He looked deep in thought. 'We've got to find a way of getting into the prop store,' he said after a moment.

The others nodded.

'We need to do it before the next show. The Angel mustn't get any more girls.'

They nodded again.

'Did anyone else hear that guard mention a contest?'

Amy and Rory nodded again. 'I don't know what he was talking about, though,' said Amy.

The Doctor jumped up. 'One way to find out!' He went back over to the theatre. The guard could still be seen in the foyer, his shadow on the window. The Doctor found a letterbox in the main door, and knelt down to it. 'Excuse me!' he called through the letterbox. 'What contest were you talking about just then?'

A few seconds later a flyer plopped out onto the pavement from the other side of the letterbox. The Doctor picked it up. 'Thank you!' he called.

He rejoined Amy and Rory. 'Aha!' he said. 'What do you think about this, then?'

Amy took the flyer from him and read it.

'Have you got what it takes? If you think you're as good as Sammy Star, come to the Britain's Got Magic try-outs. Show your tricks to TV judges Austin Hart, Daisy Mead and Bill Evans. With special guest judge, Sammy Star.'

'So?' said Rory. 'It's a thing for daft people

who want to get on telly.'

'Yes,' agreed the Doctor. 'The thing is, though, the try-outs are tomorrow, and they're at this theatre.'

'Right!' Amy got it. 'You mean you're going to enter?'

'Not quite,' said the Doctor. 'I mean, *we're* going to enter. Just call us daft people who want to get on telly. We're just going to rescue a few damsels in distress at the same time.'

Chapter Six

The Doctor, Rory and Amy were making plans.

'We have to go to the try-outs in disguise,' the Doctor said. 'Sammy Star might spot us. So might that guard, if he's around. Even if I take my cool hat off.'

'I'd suggest taking your cool hat off anyway,' said Amy. 'You know, just in case.'

'I've seen those programmes on TV,' said Rory. 'People queue up for hours to get in. We'll have to get there really early in the morning.'

'No, *we'll* have to get there really early in the morning,' the Doctor told him.

Rory looked puzzled. 'Er, that's what I said.'

'No,' the Doctor told him. 'You said "we" meaning you, me and Amy. I said "we" meaning just me and Amy. I've got another job for you, Rory.'

He told the others what he had in mind. Rory would go to the Golden Years Home for the Elderly. There he'd talk to Kylie Collins and Amber Hooper and find out all they knew about Sammy Star. Meanwhile, he and Amy would disguise themselves and go to the theatre. Once inside, they'd find out where the Weeping Angel was being kept.

'What do we do when we find it?' Amy asked.

'Good question,' said the Doctor. '*Great* question, in fact.' He stopped.

'So what's the answer to my great question?' said Amy.

The Doctor looked slightly sheepish. 'Well, I'm sure I'll have worked out something by then. We'll have a whole day to sort it out. Rory, make sure you're back by the evening for the show.'

'Right,' said Rory. 'You can count on me.'

'Good,' said the Doctor. 'Because I have a feeling we're going to need all the help we can get.'

*

The next morning, Rory caught a tube then a train and made his way to the Golden Years Home for the Elderly.

He hadn't been keen on Miss Leake, but was quite glad when she opened the door. At least she knew who he was.

'I was, er, just passing,' he said stiffly. He didn't like telling even little white lies. 'So I thought I'd pop in and see how Mrs Collins and Mrs Hooper are today.'

Miss Leake beamed at him. 'Oh, it's the nice young man from last night! Well now, aren't you sweet? Come on through, they'll be so thrilled!'

She led him into a large room. High-backed chairs were all around the edge, each with a tiny table next to it. Every chair held an elderly person, and every table held a cup of tea. A TV set blared in one corner, but no one was watching it. They were all staring ahead at nothing. Although the sun shone brightly, the French windows onto the garden remained firmly shut.

'Mrs Hooper! Mrs Collins! I've brought a visitor for you!' shouted Miss Leake. 'Isn't that nice? They're very pleased to see you,' she added to Rory, although they hadn't even looked at him.

'Er, I'll be OK from here,' Rory said, hoping to get rid of her. To his relief, she just patted his hand and left the room.

He went over to the two elderly ladies, who were sitting next to each other. Not seeing any spare seats, Rory moved an empty cup and sat on the table between them. Then he stood up again. 'This is silly,' he said. 'Let's go into the garden.'

Mrs Hooper and Mrs Collins looked as though he'd suggested bunking off school. For a second, he saw the cheeky schoolgirls they'd been once. Of course, if the Doctor was right, these old ladies had been schoolgirls only a few months ago.

Rory opened the French windows and helped the two ladies over the step into the garden. They all sat down on a little bench by a rose bed.

'It's lovely out here,' said Rory. 'You ought to come outside more. Not just sit indoors.'

'There's no point,' said Mrs Hooper dully.

Mrs Collins raised her face to the sun. 'It makes me think of being young,' she said.

'What happened when you were young?' asked Rory softly. 'Can you tell me?'

She shut her eyes, letting the sun play on her eyelids. 'We got lost,' she said.

'Lost,' Mrs Hooper echoed. 'We were so lost.'

'That's what I want you to tell me about,' said Rory. 'I want to hear about the time you were lost. It was Sammy Star, wasn't it? It was him who sent you back in time.'

There was silence. Rory didn't want to rush them, but after a few seconds asked again. 'Was it Sammy Star who sent you back in time?'

Mrs Hooper gave a loud gulp. Rory looked at her, and found to his horror that she was crying. Both old ladies were crying, huge, choking sobs. 'Please don't cry!' he said helplessly.

Mrs Collins smiled. In fact, Rory could now see that they were both smiling through the tears. He was surprised. 'You're not upset?' he asked.

'It was real, then...' Mrs Collins whispered. 'It really happened.'

'We're not mad!' said Mrs Hooper. 'We were never mad!'

'Of course you're not mad,' said Rory. 'If you knew some of the things I'd seen... No, you're really not mad. It really happened, all of it.'

'We had to forget,' Mrs Hooper went on. 'We could never talk about it. It felt like it was a dream from long ago.'

'You saw Sammy Star, though,' said Rory. 'Miss Leake said you saw the poster and kept talking about him. You knew who he was, didn't you?'

'He was just part of a dream. Someone we

might have seen long ago. Then the dream came true.'

Rory leant forward. 'Please will you try to think back? It could really help.'

'So long ago.' Mrs Hooper shook her head. 'It was so long ago. We had to forget...'

It was long ago for them, Rory knew, but it was happening right now too. Somehow he had to get them to recall the past. It might save some other girl from going through the same thing.

He had a sudden thought. The MISSING poster of Amber Reynolds. He didn't think he'd given it back to the Doctor. Had he folded it up and put it in his pocket? Yes! There it was. He pulled out the poster and unfolded it. Then he handed the paper to Mrs Hooper.

'Amber Reynolds,' he said. 'Was that you?'

She put out a nervous hand but stopped, seeming too scared to touch the picture. 'Reynolds,' she whispered. 'That was my name before I married Albert.'

'Think back,' said Rory softly. 'Think back to who you were then. To what happened to you.'

Mrs Hooper wiped her tears away. Then, after taking a deep breath, she spoke. 'It was Max.'

Rory was puzzled. He'd not heard of a Max. Was this Max in league with Sammy Star? 'What did Max do?' he asked.

She smiled. 'Oh, he was so lovely. He would run up and give me a great big lick when I came home from school.'

'Oh, Max was your *dog*!' said Rory in relief as he figured it out.

'I loved him so much. He was my only friend. Dad hit me. Mum let him. Max cared, though. He loved me as much as I loved him. Then...'

'Yes?' Rory asked, as she paused.

'Then my dad sold him. That was the thing that made me run away. He was my dog and my friend, and my dad sold him. A stranger came to the door and offered him loads of money for Max, and my dad said yes.'

'That's awful,' said Rory.

She nodded. 'I thought I could earn lots of money in London. Then I could find the stranger somehow and buy Max back. Instead I got... lost. I never saw Max again. I hope he was happy.' Tears ran down her cheeks again and this time she didn't brush them away.

Rory gave her a few moments with her long-ago grief. Then he asked, 'What happened then? What went on when you got to London?'

She didn't answer. 'Please,' he tried again. 'I have to know. The Doctor's counting on me to find out.'

'The Doctor?' said Mrs Hooper at last. 'I think I met a doctor. Back then. Back in the dream.'

'No,' said Rory. 'This isn't *a* doctor – it's *the* Doctor. Not someone you see when you're ill.'

'I thought he was mad,' she said, not taking any notice. 'Him and the red-haired girl. Both of them, mad.' She sighed. 'They were the last people I saw before I was lost.'

Rory didn't like the sound of that at all. A mad doctor and a mad red-headed girl. That just had to be the Doctor and Amy. That meant that the young Amber Reynolds was still out there somewhere. She hadn't been sent back in time yet.

Whatever the Doctor was up to, it seemed as though his plan was doomed to fail.

Miss Leake came out into the garden. She had a folded magazine under one arm and was carrying a cup. 'I wondered where you were!' she said. 'All of you out here, now mind you don't catch the sun.' She handed the cup to Rory. 'I just knew you'd like a nice cup of tea.'

Rory thanked her, even though he didn't want a cup of tea

'See, they're fine this morning after a good night's sleep,' Miss Leake carried on. She didn't seem to mind that the people she was talking about were in front of her. Waving the magazine at the two women, she said, 'Look, that nice Sammy Star's going to be on TV soon!' She turned back to Rory. 'They'll enjoy that. It'll make up for all the silly upset at the show yesterday.'

Rory didn't agree, but he nodded. He wanted her to leave so he could find out more from Mrs Hooper. Then, as she tucked the magazine back under her arm, he noticed a photo on the open page. It showed Sammy Star in front of a gravestone, holding an apple. 'Could I just have a look at that, please?' he asked, taking it from her before she could answer.

He read the first few lines. 'Oh no,' he said. 'Now we're really in trouble.'

Chapter Seven

The Doctor had rooted through the TARDIS wardrobe for costumes. He was now wearing a frilly white shirt with ruffles, and a long floppy black bow-tie. He'd swapped his tweed jacket for a velvet one. Over the top he wore a black cape with red satin lining and arm-hole slits. 'Do I look like a magician?' he asked Amy as he posed in front of a mirror.

'Very magic,' she said. 'The trousers are a bit long, though.'

'Well, I was quite a lot taller when I last wore this outfit,' he said. 'Now come on, try yours on.'

Amy held up the sparkly silver one-piece catsuit. 'I think it's a bit small for me,' she said.

'Nonsense! You'll just have to show your ankles,' the Doctor told her. 'It's perfect for Amy Pond, the magician's helper.'

Amy went behind a screen and began to change. 'Yeah, why do I have to be the helper?' she said. 'Why can't I do the magic?'

'All right,' said the Doctor, rather to her surprise. 'You do the magic then.' He paused. 'How many magic tricks do you know?'

Amy popped her head round the screen. 'None,' she said, 'as you're well aware. How many tricks do you know?'

The Doctor produced a large bunch of silk flowers from up one sleeve and handed it to her. 'Loads!'

'OK,' she said in a mock-grumpy voice. 'You win. You do the magic.' She emerged from behind the screen and did a twirl.

The Doctor picked up a dark wig and plonked it on her head. 'There. Perfect.'

'Should we come up with a plan?' Amy asked the Doctor. 'Are we just going to go on stage and make it up as we go along?'

'Making things up as we go along is what I do best,' said the Doctor. 'Oh, all right, we'll plan ahead. Just this once.' He searched through a pile of stuff and came up with a large carpet bag. 'OK, let's collect up all the things we need. Chains, sack, handcuffs, large wooden box...'

It took about half an hour, but in the end they found all the things the Doctor wanted. 'They'll never fit in that bag,' Amy said, looking at the man-size wooden cabinet. The

Doctor told her that the bag was bigger on the inside than the outside, and pushed the things in one by one. Once all the items were inside, even the cabinet, he shut the clasp of the carpet bag with a loud *snap*.

'I'm glad I got this back from Mary Poppins,' he said. 'Shall we go?'

'Hang on,' said Amy, ' I don't suppose you've got another bag like that, have you? Handbag-sized. You know what it's like, lipstick, hankie, sunglasses, keys and then there's no room for the kitchen sink.'

The Doctor delved into the heap of things again, then handed her a tiny shoulder bag.

'Ooh, silver to match,' she said. She put her sunglasses and sun lotion into the bag. Then the Doctor's bunch of silk flowers, and a silk scarf. Then she tried to fit in a hat stand but couldn't manage it. 'Oh well, you can't have it all,' she said with a shrug.

'Ready now?' asked the Doctor, pretending to look at a watch.

Amy grinned. 'Yes, I'm ready!'

'Well, then, come along, Pond – let's make magic!'

*

The queue was already halfway round Trafalgar Square when the Doctor and Amy arrived. People of all shapes, sizes and ages were waiting to get in. Some were dressed in normal clothes. Some wore top hats or spangly outfits. One wore a tiger costume.

They joined the end of the line. In front of them, a man in glasses was working on card tricks. Next to him, a girl was trying to keep hold of a squirming rabbit.

'What's your act, then, mate?' asked a man with a top hat on his head.

'I escape,' said the Doctor.

The man sniffed. 'Been at it long?'

'Hmm.' The Doctor thought about it for a second. 'About a thousand years. Give or take a century or so. Escape, capture, escape, capture, pretty much the story of my lives.'

'Yeah, I know what you mean, mate,' the top-hatted man agreed.

By the time the theatre opened its doors, the end of the queue was out of sight. 'I hope we're not out here too long,' Amy said, popping on her sunglasses. 'I'm cooking like a Christmas turkey in tinfoil in this silver get-up. The wig's making my head sweat, too.'

'Thanks for sharing that,' said the Doctor. Amy wrinkled her nose at him.

People started to go into the theatre through one door. After about ten minutes, the first people left again by another door. They all looked upset. The man in the tiger suit was crying.

'Get a life!' Amy whispered to the Doctor. 'Crying because you don't get on a TV show, that's pretty sad.'

'Be kind,' said the Doctor. 'Some people don't know there's a whole universe out there.'

'Well, they should try finding out,' said Amy.

It was some time before the Doctor and Amy got to the doors of the theatre. A guard was standing outside, stopping people getting in before they were wanted. To Amy's relief, it wasn't the guard they'd met the night before. She wasn't sure their disguises were really good enough to fool anyone. People tended not to forget the Doctor.

After a few more minutes, the guard waved them into the foyer.

A man with a clipboard came up to them. He handed them a piece of card with a number on it. 'You will be shown into the theatre. When your number is called you will go on the stage. The judges and Sammy Star will be sitting in the front row. You may begin when they tell you to. Your act should take no more than three minutes. The judges may stop you and ask you to leave at any point. Got that?'

'Yes, sir!' said Amy, giving him a salute. 'Has he been taking lessons from the Daleks?' she whispered to the Doctor.

They had to sign a form. Amy spotted that the Doctor had signed it 'Fred Astaire', so she signed it 'Ginger Rogers'. The man didn't seem to notice. He ushered them in to the main theatre and went to tell the rules to the next person.

A short, stocky girl in top hat and tails was on the stage. 'Just one more trick,' she pleaded, taking her hat off her head and pulling some flags out of it.

'Thank you, we've seen quite enough,' someone said from the stalls. 'That's a No from me.'

Amy peered into the seats. She'd seen the three judges on TV before. That voice belonged to Austin Hart, a tall, smug-looking man covered in fake tan. Next to him was Bill Evans who was short, bald and Welsh. The only woman in the line-up was Daisy Mead, a model who'd married a pop star.

'Enough for a life time,' said Bill Evans. 'Don't give up the day job, love. No from me.'

Daisy Mead drawled, 'I don't want to be cruel, right? It was just dreadful though. Really bad.'

'So that's a hat-trick of "No"s for your hat trick,' sniggered Austin Hart. 'Sammy? Do you have any comments to add?'

'Learning magic is hard work,' said Sammy Star. 'It's also lonely.' The girl on stage nodded. 'For some people it's worth it. For you, it isn't. You're awful.'

The girl burst into tears. She put the hat back on her head, flags hanging over her ears.

Amy turned to the Doctor. 'That's really mean. Do they have to be so nasty? So her magic's not great. What have they done with *their* lives?'

The Doctor's eyes narrowed. 'For some people, being mean to others is the point of their lives. They're the ones you should be feeling sorry for. It must be worse than being a Cyberman.'

As the girl shuffled off the stage, a voice called 'Number thirty-seven, please.'

'Ooh, that's us!' said the Doctor. He nudged Amy, and led her onto the stage.

'Name?' asked Austin Hart.

'I'm Doctor Daring,' said the Doctor giving them a wave, 'and this is the Amazing Amy, my lovely helper.' Amy smiled and did a twirl.

'What's your act?'

The Doctor bowed. 'I am an escape artist. In fact, I am the best escape artist you will ever see.'

All four of the judges started laughing.

The Doctor turned to Amy. 'You know, I think they might be laughing *at* us, rather than laughing *with* us. That's not very nice.'

'Well, let's give them something to laugh about,' said Amy, opening the carpet bag. She pulled out the chains with a flourish and began to wind them around the Doctor. Next out of the bag came three huge padlocks. She displayed them to the watchers, then linked them through the chains. One by one, she snapped them shut.

The Doctor wriggled his fingers, showing he was held firm by the chains. Amy faced him and raised her eyebrows. He gave a slight nod. That was their signal to show the bonds were loose enough for him. He had to seem trapped, but still be able to reach his sonic screwdriver.

So far things were going as planned. Amy pulled a sack out of the bag and placed it over the Doctor's head. He gave her a wink before the cloth covered his face. She then produced a large wooden cabinet from the bag. Although such a big box could never have fitted in a bag of that size, no one clapped. Amy almost laughed. The judges thought an alien wonder was just a cheap trick! They really were clueless.

Getting the box into the right place was the most crucial part of the Doctor's plan. He'd told Amy just where it had to be placed on the stage. She had to be careful while looking careless. The watchers mustn't guess that she was putting the cabinet on top of a trapdoor.

Certain it was in the right place, Amy stepped away from the box. She tapped it hard on all sides to show it was solid. Then she ushered the bound Doctor into it. Using handcuffs, she fixed him to metal rings inside the box. When it was clear that the Doctor was helpless, she shut the door on him.

For Amy, the next few minutes would be tricky. All eyes were on her, and she had to keep it that way. The Doctor needed all the time she could buy him.

'Trapped in this box!' she cried. 'How will he escape his bonds?'

The seconds ticked past slowly as she danced around the cabinet. Whenever she was behind it, out of sight of the judges, she rattled a piece of chain. That would make people think the Doctor was trying to escape inside the box.

At last someone called out, 'Three minutes are up.'

'Just a bit longer!' she called back. She put her ear to the box, acting as if she could hear a voice from inside. 'He's nearly free!'

'Do us a favour, love!' said Bill Evans. 'You're wasting our time.'

'Well spotted. That's the point,' muttered Amy to herself.

'You're going to have to let him out now,' said Austin, sounding bored.

'I am, like, so asleep already,' said Daisy Mead.

Amy smiled and pretended to try the door. 'It's stuck!' she said. 'Hold on, give me a moment.' She made a show of pulling the handle. 'No, really stuck. Sorry!'

'Hang on a minute,' came an angry voice. 'I know that accent.' Sammy Star jumped up from his seat and stormed onto the stage. Amy ducked round behind the box. She was able to waste quite a few more seconds as Sammy Star chased her round and round.

The judges cheered from the stalls. 'This is the best thing we've seen yet!' called Austin Hart.

It couldn't go on for ever, of course. Sammy Star caught up with Amy and grabbed hold of her wig. 'Aha! I thought so!' he cried as her long red hair tumbled out. 'The Scottish redhead from last night! She's a spy,' he told the judges. 'She's trying to ruin my act, her and this Doctor Daring friend of hers.'

'Yeah, but he's, like, stuck in that box, yeah?' said Daisy Mead. 'So he's not doing anything, is he?'

Sammy Star hissed through his teeth. He shoved Amy out of the way and opened the box.

It was empty.

'Oh, sorry, did we say this was an escape act? It's really a disappearing act,' said Amy. She grinned. 'Our mistake.'

Chapter Eight

As soon as Amy shut the door of the box, the Doctor set to work. He'd hidden the sonic screwdriver up his sleeve, and now he shook it down into his hand. Amy had been careful to leave the chains loose enough to allow him to do that.

A couple of quick buzzes from the screwdriver made the chains and padlocks fall away, followed by the handcuffs. The Doctor pulled the sack off his head and knelt down.

He'd watched Sammy Star's act closely. Sammy had appeared from a 'grave' as if by magic. The Doctor had worked out that there must be a trapdoor in the stage. He'd told Amy to put the cabinet over that exact spot. Now he opened the trapdoor and climbed down.

There was just enough space to stand up under the stage. He shut the trapdoor behind him, then looked around. A dim light showed a door to one side. The Doctor went through it and found himself in the heart of the theatre. There were no guards or dogs as no intruder was supposed to get this far in. This was the place he'd been searching for, Sammy Star's prop store.

There was a keypad by the storeroom door. A sequence of numbers would be needed to unlock it.

Just as he was about to attack the lock with the sonic screwdriver, he heard movement. There was someone inside the room. It couldn't be Sammy Star, as he was still upstairs in the theatre. The Doctor shrugged and knocked on the door. It seemed the easiest way.

'Who is it?' a girl's voice called from inside the room.

'It's me,' the Doctor called back. He'd noticed before that people often accepted that without asking who 'me' was.

Sure enough, the door was opened from inside. A girl stood there. She had long black hair and wore a white Victorian-style nightdress. The Doctor did a double-take, but a second look showed it wasn't Kylie Duncan. She was in the past now, the Doctor knew. It must be that Sammy Star chose girls who looked alike. That way people wouldn't notice it was a new girl every night.

'Hello?' said the girl.

'Hello, I'm the Doctor,' replied the Doctor

cheerfully. He shut the door behind him and was inside the room before she knew what had happened.

He looked around with interest. A cage in a corner held a large, sad white rabbit with floppy ears. Plastic gravestones leant against the walls. There was a full-length mirror on a stand. Chains and ropes dangled from hooks. A dozen costumes hung from a rail.

Next to the rabbit's cage was a tall box. It was about the same size and shape as the one he'd been locked in. He smiled, thinking of Amy still dancing around on the stage.

As the girl watched, confused, he ran the sonic screwdriver across the box. 'Hmm,' he said, glancing at a reading. 'Lead-lined.'

'No one's allowed to touch that box!' the girl cried. 'That's why the door was locked!'

'Well, yes, he would have told you that,' said the Doctor. 'Wouldn't want anything to happen to you before tonight, would he?'

'What do you mean?'

The Doctor stared straight at her. 'We're going to have a little talk in a minute. Then you're going to leave. You're in danger here.'

'I was in danger out there, Doctor Whoever-you-are,' she said. 'It's not much fun being on the streets. This bloke's offering me a good job, good money, a chance of being on the telly.'

'Where you'll end up, there isn't any telly!' the Doctor told her. 'They stopped broadcasts during the war and it doesn't begin again until 1946. Even then it's pretty much only Muffin the Mule and the News!'

'You're mad,' the girl said.

'Yes, yes, yes,' said the Doctor. 'Now, are you going to help me steal this box or not?'

She stared at him. 'Not, of course!' She turned away. 'I'm going to get Mr Star.'

He darted across the room to get to the door first. 'Please don't,' he said, barring her way. 'I'll explain.' He took a deep breath.

The door burst open, nearly hitting the Doctor, and Sammy Star charged in. 'I knew it!' he said. 'I knew I'd find you here!' He turned to the girl. 'Go and wait in the theatre while I deal with this spy.'

'I'm not a spy,' said the Doctor as the girl hurried out. 'I'm a concerned citizen. Concerned that you've got a deadly alien monster inside that box, and you keep letting it loose.'

'I don't care if it's deadly,' said Sammy Star. 'I don't care if it's alien and I don't care if it's a monster. All I care is that it's bringing me

72

fame and fortune. I'm not going to let you spoil that for me.'

The Doctor boggled. 'You're really putting fame and fortune above the lives of all these young girls?'

'Yes.' The magician strode towards him. 'They're nothing. They're worthless. The scum of the gutter. They have no place, no use. They have no home.'

'I have no home,' said the Doctor quietly. 'Having no home doesn't make you a lesser person.' He turned and pointed at the lead-lined box. 'Doing this sort of thing is what makes you a lesser person.'

The Doctor shouldn't have turned his back. Sammy Star grabbed a coil of rope off a hook and jumped on him. The Doctor fought back, but he'd been taken by surprise. His arms were pinned to his sides, and Sammy Star tied him to a chair.

'No one's going to get in my way,' the man said. 'I don't know how this thing works, but I know that it *does* work.' He unlocked the padlock on the lead-lined box and nudged the door open. 'I'll say goodbye now.' He backed out of the room and the Doctor heard the sound of a beep as the door locked itself.

He'd dropped the sonic screwdriver during

the struggle. It took just a fraction of a second for him to look down to see where it had landed. By the time he looked up again, the Weeping Angel was out of the box.

'Oh dear,' the Doctor murmured to himself. 'This is slightly awkward.'

*

Amy was carried out of the theatre by a security guard.

'Wow,' said a girl who was dressed as a court jester. 'I thought it was bad when they came out crying.'

Amy wasn't surprised to be thrown out. It was getting to be a habit. She only hoped that the ruse had bought the Doctor enough time. He would have had a couple of minutes' head start, at least. As long as he was able to find the Angel, that was the main thing. They had a good few hours yet to work out how to deal with it. Of course, she also had to work out a way of getting back into the theatre. At least she had a while to sort that out too.

She went and sat by one of the bronze lions in Trafalgar Square while she thought things through.

Amy wasn't sure how long she'd been sitting there when she heard a vehicle screech to a halt. A minibus had stopped on one of the roads at the edge of Trafalgar Square. To her huge surprise, she saw Rory jump out of its door. To her even greater surprise, two old ladies hobbled after him, walking sticks in hands. They appeared to be the two old women who'd sat behind them in the theatre the night before.

'Hey! Hey! Over here!' Amy called out.

Rory heard and swerved towards her. 'Nice outfit,' he began.

'Yes, yes, yes,' said Amy. 'I look like I'm from the space year 3000, I know. What are you doing here? I think you're going to get a parking ticket, by the way.'

'I found out something. I thought the Doctor ought to know as soon as possible,' Rory said. The two ladies joined them. 'Amy, this is Kylie Duncan and Amber Reynolds, as was. Now Mrs Collins and Mrs Hooper.'

'Hello, we met last night,' said Amy. 'It's very nice to see you.'

Mrs Hooper peered at her. 'You tied me up.'

'Er, no,' Amy said. 'I'm pretty sure you're thinking of someone else there.' She quickly turned to Rory. 'What is it that the Doctor needs to know?'

'Oh, right. Yes.' Rory frowned. 'OK. This

is what it is. We were talking in the garden, and Miss Leake came out. She's the warden of the Golden Years home. Anyway, she had a magazine. I didn't realise what it meant at first.'

'What *what* meant?' Amy was almost shouting. 'Come on, come on!'

'There was an interview with Sammy Star. It said he's being filmed this afternoon, while those talent-show judges are here. He's being filmed doing the Graveyard Ghost act, then it's being shown on TV later. We thought we had hours, but the Angel could be let loose any time now. We've got to tell the Doctor before it sends some other poor girl back into the past!'

Amy stared at him in horror. 'It's much worse than that,' she said.

Pictures from a long time ago flashed into her mind. She'd been locked in a room. A recording of a Weeping Angel had started to come to life before her eyes.

'The image of an Angel itself becomes an Angel,' she whispered, hardly daring to say the words out loud. 'So if a Weeping Angel is filmed and shown on TV...'

She couldn't carry on. The thought was just too scary. A Weeping Angel would appear in front of each TV set that was showing Sammy Star's act. Millions of Weeping Angels coming to life all over the country. Perhaps all over the world.

Chapter Nine

The Doctor was struggling. He was struggling to get out of his bonds and he was struggling not to blink. He knew his eyes had flickered once or twice already. In those tiny moments, the Angel had advanced. It was halfway across the room now.

The big mirror on its stand was at the other end of the room. The Doctor could see himself in it out of the corner of his eye. He looked helpless, and that was making him angry. He struggled even harder.

'I wouldn't bother zapping me if I were you,' he told the Angel. 'You feed on the energy of the time I would have had in the future. Well, I'm still going to have it. I'm not human, you see. I'll just live out a few decades and then pop right through that door.' He paused for a second, hoping to hear the door open. It didn't happen. Of course, he couldn't turn up and rescue himself before he'd been sent back in time. If that happened, he wouldn't have got sent back in time after all and so couldn't rescue himself. It was confusing, even for a Time Lord.

'I'm almost looking forward to it,' the Doctor said. 'Bit of a break. Chance to catch up with a few old friends as I go through the years. Winston Churchill. Agatha Christie. The Beatles.'

He knew the Angel was stone at that moment, but could've sworn it glared at him.

There were footsteps outside the door. Could this be it? Was the future him about to walk into the room? Meeting himself was always odd.

Beep beep beep beep. That was the correct sequence of numbers being entered onto the keypad. The door opened...

'Hey, what's this?' said a gruff voice. In the mirror, the Doctor saw a thickset man in blue overalls. It didn't take him long to decide it wasn't himself – not even in a new body.

A second man came in. 'Star said that Angel statue might be out of its box,' he said. 'He didn't say anything about a bloke tied to a chair, did he, Ted?'

'Yes, hello,' said the Doctor, not taking his eyes off the Angel. 'Speaking as the bloke tied to the chair, could you untie me please?'

The first man, Ted, laughed. 'Not likely!

Star's always saying we're not to touch a thing in here unless he tells us to. You'll be one of his magic friends trying out a trick.'

If the Doctor could have turned his head, he would have given the man a hard stare. He had to be content with glaring at the mirror instead. 'I'm not one of Sammy Star's magic friends. I'm not even one of his non-magic friends. You have to believe me that we're all in great danger. Please let me go.'

Ted laughed again. 'Nah, it's all a trick, isn't it? Come on, Larry. Let's get the statue back in its box.'

'No!' the Doctor almost screamed at them. 'Don't go near that thing! It's a monster!'

Larry nodded. 'You're right, it's not very pretty. Dunno how he gets it to move around like that. There again, if I knew his secrets, I'd be the one about to go on telly.'

'Telly?' cried the Doctor. 'What telly? Who's going on telly? DON'T BLOCK MY VIEW!'

Ted had moved in between the Doctor and the Angel. To the Doctor's relief, either Ted or Larry had still got their eyes on it. It remained a statue.

The two men picked up the Angel and carried it back into its lead-lined box. The door closed on it. The Doctor thought he heard a movement inside at the very instant it was hidden from view.

'Got to get it on stage,' Larry told the Doctor. 'Mr Star's graveyard trick's going to be on telly. The film crew's already setting up upstairs. Good luck with your trick, mate.'

'I'm not doing a trick!' the Doctor told them. 'I'm tied to this chair so I can't stop Sammy Star doing a very bad thing. A very bad thing indeed. I can't really explain it to you because you won't believe me. You just have to trust me. Let me go now!'

'Ha ha, good one, mate,' said Ted. 'Come along, Larry.' They carried the box out of the door, and shut it behind them.

The Doctor was left to struggle with his bonds again. He knew as well as Amy did what would happen if the Angel was shown on TV. It could be the end of the world.

*

'We have to warn the Doctor,' said Amy. 'There's got to be a way of getting back inside the theatre.'

Rory nodded. 'There is. I'm just going to walk in.'

'Er, yeah, right!' said Amy. 'I don't think that's going to work.'

'Why not?' Rory was sure of himself for

once. 'Only one guard saw me, and he didn't really look at me. I don't stand out like you. You know, tall, pretty, red hair,' he said in a hurry as Amy frowned at him. 'Not to mention dressed in a one-piece silver catsuit. It's a look people notice. They won't look at me twice. I'm going to say Mrs Collins or Mrs Hooper left a bag under a seat last night and can I go and get it.'

'We'll come with you,' said Mrs Collins. 'They'll believe you then.'

Amy turned to her. 'Are you sure? It might be dangerous.'

The old woman smiled. 'For the past few years I've barely known my own name, dear. Today I feel young again. If I can help stop Sammy Star, I'm going to.'

Mrs Hooper didn't say anything. She was staring at Amy. 'It *was* you,' she said.

'Er, no, it wasn't,' said Amy. 'Really.' She quickly turned back to Rory. 'Every second could count. You've got to get in there and find the Doctor.'

'Right.' Rory and the two old ladies headed off for the theatre.

Amy watched as they spoke to the man at the door. To her relief, they were let in. It wasn't in Amy's nature to stand around waiting for other people to do the work. She knew she couldn't get into the theatre by the front door. That didn't mean she couldn't find some other way in.

She thought back to the time she'd climbed onto the stage. Sammy Star had thought she wanted him to sign her programme. He'd told her to wait at the stage door. Perhaps it would be easier to get in there.

She made her way to the back of the theatre. There were no neon signs or grand entrances here, just dustbins and pigeons. Even the sun stayed out of the gloomy alley.

Amy grinned despite the gloom. She'd spotted something that made her very happy. A lorry was parked beside the alley. Men were lifting down heavy cameras and lights and carrying them to the stage door. It was the TV crew.

She waited until the last man was out of the lorry, then jumped inside. Someone had left a denim jacket lying around, and she put it on. It didn't hide all of her silver catsuit, but might fool someone at a quick glance. There was a handheld camera on the floor. She picked it up. Carried on her shoulder, it hid her face. Then, trying to look very sure of herself, she walked straight through the stage door.

'Down there on the left,' a voice called. She thought she'd better do as it said. To her surprise, she found herself near the side of the stage. The Graveyard Ghost set was already in place. Sammy Star and the other judges were still sitting at the front of the stalls. Amy hurried towards the back of the hall in case they turned and saw her. The cameras and lights were being set up nearby.

At the back of the theatre sat a girl. A girl with long black hair, dressed in a white nightie. All of a sudden, Amy knew what she had to do. There was no sign of the Doctor or Rory. This could all be up to her.

The denim jacket had a pass clipped to a pocket. It read CREW. Amy went over to the girl and waved the pass in front of her nose. 'Excuse me, you're needed in make-up. Can you come with me, please?'

The girl followed Amy out of a side exit. Above the door was an arrow pointing to LADIES.

'Just in here,' Amy said, at the end of the passage.

'The dressing rooms are downstairs,' said the girl, puzzled.

'Not today. They've taken over the ladies' loos,' said Amy, and shoved her inside. 'Come on, come on, let's have that nightie off you.'

'You what?' said the girl.

'Costume check,' said Amy. The girl didn't look convinced, but took it off. She was now dressed only in T-shirt and leggings.

'I'll have the wig too, please,' Amy said. She plucked it off the girl's head, revealing blonde hair underneath. 'Bet it feels better without it. Wigs really make your head sweaty, don't they?'

The blonde girl frowned. 'Are you really with Wardrobe? I'm going to go and check with Sammy.'

She tried to get to the door, but Amy held her fast. Amy realised she had a scarf in her shoulder bag. On her first attempt she pulled out the bunch of silk flowers, but she searched further and found the scarf. She whipped it out and tied the struggling girl's hands to a pipe. There was a hankie in her borrowed jacket's pocket, and she used it as a gag.

'I'm sorry,' she said. 'Really I am. Believe me, though, this is a lot better than what Sammy Star had planned for you.' Then she grinned. 'You know what? This reminds me of one of the first times I met the Doctor. I handcuffed him to a pipe. Hang on a minute. Have we met before?'

For a moment, Amy had thought the blonde girl looked familiar. The girl just glared at her, though, and didn't answer.

Amy put on the nightie and wig. Once dressed, she looked at herself in the mirror. 'Perfect,' she said. 'All ready to be scared by the Graveyard Ghosts.'

Except tonight, Amy told herself, it would be the ghosts' turn to be scared.

Chapter Ten

Rory and the two old ladies went through the door marked NO ENTRANCE. There were no guards to be seen, but as they crept further in Rory heard a dog bark.

'Uh-oh,' he said. 'I thought the Doctor was joking when he said about guard dogs.'

Mrs Hooper's face lit up. 'It's all right,' she said. 'It's nothing to worry about.'

'Er, if you say so,' said Rory, not at all sure that she was right.

Round a corner, there were the dogs. Two big German Shepherds. To Rory's surprise, they stopped barking as Mrs Hooper went up to them. They even started to lick her outstretched hand.

'This is Brandy and this is Lady,' she said. 'I made friends with them. I was missing Max so much.'

'Oh!' All of a sudden Rory figured it out. 'You made friends with them when you were in the theatre before. When you were young. To the dogs, I guess you still smell like the same person!'

Mrs Hooper didn't want to leave the dogs, but they had to go on. Rory stopped a bit further along. 'Did you hear something?' he asked. He listened again. Yes, there it was. A voice was calling. It was the Doctor's voice!

'Don't worry, Doctor, we'll get you out!' Rory shouted back as he reached the door. Then he stopped. 'The door's locked,' he called to the Doctor.

'Yes, I know that,' the Doctor's voice came back.

'Do you know the code that opens it?' asked Rory. 'There's a keypad here.'

'No,' came the Doctor's reply. 'Come on, come on, Rory! A four digit number, there are only ten thousand possible ones. Get those fingers working!'

'Er, OK,' said Rory. He touched the keypad. 0000. Nothing. 0001. Nothing. 0002. Nothing. 'This might take a little time,' he said.

A wrinkled hand reached out and pushed his hand aside. A wrinkled finger punched in the numbers 2906. The door clicked open.

'The 29th of June,' said Mrs Collins. 'My birthday. I noticed that the code was my birthday. It's all coming back to me now. Being here again.'

Inside the room, Rory began to untie the Doctor. Mrs Collins and Mrs Hooper were looking past him. As if in a dream, they walked towards the mirror. Mrs Collins reached out a hand and touched her image. The image's fingers met hers.

'So old,' she said in wonder. 'We got so old. I was young when I was in this room before. Young and pretty. Scared but so full of hope.'

Mrs Hooper nodded. 'My hair was long and golden. I didn't like hiding it with a wig, but he said I had to. This room... I was waiting in this room. Waiting to go on the stage. They were going to film it. I was going to be famous. Then a mad man came in and spoilt it all. That man there.' She pointed at the Doctor. 'It all happened in my dream. The red-haired girl was in my dream too. She stole my clothes and took my place. I was so angry. Then suddenly I was so lost.'

Rory and the Doctor listened with horror. 'That was you!' said the Doctor. 'The girl I met here, today, that was you!'

That wasn't the bit Rory latched on to. 'The red-haired girl took your place?' he said. 'Doctor, it's Amy! She's taking part in Sammy Star's act!'

The Doctor threw off the last of his bonds

and jumped up. 'She's up there with a Weeping Angel!'

*

The Weeping Angel was on stage. Two men had taken it out of a large box and put it in its place. Sammy Star had walked past Amy as she stood in the wings, watching. 'I'm off to get changed,' he'd said. 'You know what you've got to do?'

She had nodded, keeping the dark hair of the wig over her face as much as she could. He didn't seem to notice she wasn't the same girl. Well, with a new girl each day, he probably couldn't keep track.

'Good,' he'd said. 'Nothing must go wrong today. I am about to get my revenge.'

That hadn't sounded good. Amy knew now more than ever that she had to foil his plans somehow. Her idea was simple. She'd go along with the act as much as she could. The only thing was, she would never take her eye off the Weeping Angel. Not for a single second.

A short while later, a voice called 'Action!'

Mist came out of a dry-ice machine and crept across the stage.

Amy had seen the show, so she knew what she had to do. She copied Kylie Duncan's movements as closely as she could.

Sammy Star, dressed as the Graveyard Ghost, emerged from his grave. Amy didn't have to pretend to be scared. There was a mad look in his eyes that was very, very scary.

She darted away from him, and spikes sprang up near her feet. She was being herded towards the tall tree that would become a walkway.

It felt real. It *was* real. The person chasing her might not be a ghost, but he wanted to hurt her.

Sammy Star was throwing apples as Amy reached the tallest tree. Its bark fell away as she began to climb. Amy had never been scared of heights, but this walkway felt really high right now. She paused for a moment, dizzy, and Sammy Star's dagger nearly went through her foot.

Up and up she climbed. Somehow she kept her eyes on the Weeping Angel below.

She was aware of a noise from down in the theatre. Someone was shouting. It might have been the Doctor, but it seemed so far away.

Higher and higher, until she could go no further. This was it. This was the end. Sammy Star was behind her. He was going to throw the apple that would knock her down. Any moment now would come the blinding flash.

With one hand, Amy reached into her bag and pulled out her pair of sunglasses.

She put on the sunglasses. The other hand reached out and caught the apple. She wobbled, but didn't fall. There was a blinding flash...

Amy, with her dark glasses on, kept looking down at the Angel.

*

The Doctor and Rory burst in, Mrs Collins and Mrs Hooper behind them. Amy was poised on the top of the walkway. 'Keep looking at the Angel!' the Doctor yelled, although he knew it was useless. He ran towards the stage as fast as he could. If he was close enough to the Angel, maybe he'd still see it through the flash. At least he'd be offering himself as a victim rather than Amy.

He couldn't run fast enough. He couldn't get there in time. Sammy Star raised his hand to throw the apple. There was a blinding flash...

When the Doctor stopped blinking, he saw that the Angel hadn't moved. Amy, still at the top of the walkway, was staring at it through her sunglasses.

'Yes! Oh, good girl, Pond!' he yelled. 'Now come on down. Mind the spikes. Tell you what,' he called to a man in the wings, 'just get rid of the spikes, will you?'

The spikes slid back down, and the Doctor climbed up. Scattered apples rolled off the stage behind him. He looked up at Sammy Star, still near the top of the walkway. The magician didn't even move as Amy made her way past him.

'Time to retire, I think,' said the Doctor.

Sammy shook his head. 'Not yet. Oh, not yet. I've barely even started.'

'She locked me in the loos!' A blonde girl ran onto the stage. The girl the Doctor had met before, the one he now knew was Amber Reynolds. 'Oi, you, what do you think you were playing at?' Amber yelled at Amy. 'I'd have been there all day if someone hadn't found me.'

'Stop!' the Doctor yelled. The girl was getting close to the Angel. 'Stay away from that!'

'*Nooooooo!*' It was like the night before all over again. The screaming of an elderly lady in the stalls. Everyone turned to look at her.

The Doctor couldn't help it. His eyes flicked away too, just for an instant.

When he looked back, the Angel had moved.

The blonde girl was gone.

Chapter Eleven

The cameras were still rolling as the judges jumped to their feet. 'We were promised a show to astound us,' said Austin Hart with a sneer. 'This is hardly such a show.'

'It's just, like, really dumb,' said Daisy Mead. 'Yawn-arama.'

Amy, now down on the stage, was again amazed. A girl had just been blasted into the past, but these judges thought it was nothing. Just because they'd been looking away when it happened.

Sammy Star called down to the judges from the top of the walkway. 'Oh, I'm going to give you a show,' he said. 'I'm going to give you a show you'll never forget. You'll be sorry for the way you laughed at me. Let's see if you're still laughing when the Angel gets you.'

The Doctor looked up. 'You don't want to do that,' he warned.

'Oh yes I do,' ranted Sammy. 'They're rude and they laugh at people and it hurts so much. I wanted what they've got! I wanted to be famous! When I found the Angel, I knew just what I had to do. I could get everything I wanted. Fame, and revenge. Austin Hart, Daisy Mead and Bill Evans being zapped into nothing? I'll be on every news channel in the world.'

'Get out of here!' shouted the Doctor. But no one moved. 'I'm talking to all of you! Every person in this theatre! Leave now!' There was a second's silence, and then people began running to the doors. The judges, the film crew, the stagehands. Only Rory, Amy and the two old ladies stayed still.

'No!' screamed Sammy Star. He was still at the top of the walkway, and was holding something in his hand. A wire trailed from it. Amy felt suddenly cold. It was the control for the pyrotechnics. She watched helplessly as the Doctor ran towards the walkway. But Sammy hit the button before the Doctor could reach it. There was a second blinding flash.

'Amy!' shouted the Doctor.

Amy was still wearing her dark glasses. But even so, she was taken by surprise. By the time she was able to focus on the Angel, it had moved.

It was right next to her. Amy gasped in horror. She was trapped at the very edge of the stage. The Angel was now blocking her only escape.

Amy had nowhere to go. 'Oh help oh help oh help,' she muttered, backing away.

Rory ran towards the stage. Mrs Collins and Mrs Hooper followed him as fast as they could.

Then there was another flash. Amy blinked. Suddenly the Angel was poised over her, its fangs bared, its hands clawing for her.

Amy was almost bent backwards to avoid its deadly touch. Somehow she managed to creep back just a little further. But now she was out of room. The next time she so much as blinked, the Angel would get her.

'Amy, look out!' Rory cried.

It was too late. Amy had moved too close to the edge of the stage. She wobbled... Then, with a cry of despair, she fell.

As she fell, a lot of things happened at once.

Something green flew past Amy. There was another blinding flash. There was a scream...

Amy picked herself up. She was shaking with fear. The Angel had moved again, and there was no trace of Sammy Star.

'What happened?' Amy asked in a trembling voice.

Rory gently put his arms around her. 'An apple,' he said. 'Someone threw an apple. Just as Sammy Star set off that firework, or whatever it was. I think I saw the apple hit him, but then I was blinded. We all were.'

'So he fell off, and the Angel got him,' said Amy. 'I tumbled off the stage, so the Angel went for the next nearest target. It was used to catching people falling off that walkway.' She looked at the Weeping Angel, now standing beneath the walkway. It was stone again. 'Who threw the apple?'

The Doctor came down the stairs at the side of the stage backwards. 'I'm not going to take my eyes off that Angel,' he said. 'I think I can tell you the answer without looking, though. You didn't expect to see yourself on stage, did you, Mrs Hooper? To see the dreadful moment when young Amber Reynolds got lost.'

'Lost,' came Mrs Hooper's shaky voice. 'I was so very lost.'

Amy had her eyes fixed on the Angel too, but she could hear that Mrs Hooper was crying.

'I was there, on stage,' said Mrs Hooper. 'All of a sudden, it didn't seem like a dream any more. It was real.'

'That was you!' Amy cried. 'The girl who

vanished. The girl who I tied up. That was you! Oh. Right. You'd already told me that, before it happened. No wonder she looked familiar. I'd seen her face on the MISSING poster. Your face, I guess I should say.'

Rory rested his hand on Mrs Hooper's arm. 'It must have been a shock to see yourself like that,' he said.

'Yes, my dear. It was a big shock, waking up from the dream. But I am awake now. You know, I wouldn't change things. I met my Albert back then, I had my lovely girls. As I woke up, though, all I could think of was Max. That was the moment when he stole Max from me. That was the moment I lost Max for ever.'

Amy hadn't thought much of Amber Reynolds the girl. Not that she'd spent a lot of time getting to know her. She thought she liked Amber Hooper the adult, though.

Rory coughed. 'Er, Doctor?'

'Yes?'

'Are we going to have to stay here for ever? I just wondered.' Rory took Amy's hand and squeezed it. 'Sammy Star might have gone, but the Angel's still here.'

'We could go and find that box,' Amy said. 'The one Sammy Star locked it in.'

The Doctor shook his head. 'That wouldn't keep it trapped for long. It was only so placid because it was getting fed every night. Let it miss a few meals and it'd soon find a way out of the box.'

'Er, Doctor,' said Rory again. 'I don't know if this is a good time to mention it, but I think the cameras are still on.'

'Oh well,' said Amy, 'I suppose it might be fun to see yourself on TV.

'I don't think so,' Rory began, then stopped, his mouth hanging open.

'What is it?' Amy asked.

'See yourself,' he said. 'See yourself! Doctor! What if the Angel saw itself in a mirror? It would be looking at itself for ever!'

'Yes!' yelled Amy, jumping up and down. 'Go Rory!'

The Doctor didn't seem so sure. 'I don't know,' he said. 'It might work. It all depends if eye contact is the main factor or just the state of being watched. Then there's the risk of something getting between the Angel and the mirror. Not to mention what might happen if it goes dark, or if the mirror gets broken...'

'Oh,' said Rory. 'I thought it was a good idea. Sorry.'

'It *is* a good idea!' Amy cried.

'No,' said the Doctor. 'I've just explained that—'

Amy cut across him. 'The image of an Angel becomes an Angel,' she said.

'Yes!' Now it was the Doctor yelling. 'That's it! Rory, I won't let anyone ever call you stupid again. Quick, there's a large mirror down in the prop room. Take Amy and bring it up here. Go on, now, chop chop. Amber and Kylie here will keep watch with me. As long as we don't all blink at once we'll be OK.'

Amy and Rory hurried away, leaving the Doctor and the two old ladies staring at the Weeping Angel. Now the theatre was empty they had no problems getting to the prop store. Even the dogs had gone.

'Right,' said the Doctor as they arrived with the mirror. 'We have to put it in just the right place. We want the Angel almost nose to nose with its image.'

The mirror was placed in front of the Weeping Angel, and they all breathed a sigh of relief.

The Doctor made a round of the cameras, zapping each with his sonic screwdriver. 'All the recordings destroyed,' he said. 'The film crew won't be happy, but I think it's better than letting the world end.'

'Yes, I think so,' said Amy with a grin.

'Now I'm just popping out for a while,' said the Doctor. 'Keep an eye on that Angel for me, will you? I'll meet you in Trafalgar Square in an hour.'

'Where are you going?' asked Amy, but the Doctor was already out of the door.

*

They waited, and watched. It was creepy. Amy was glad she had Rory's hand to hold. Not that she was going to tell him that.

An image flickered on the far side of the mirror, and Amy shivered. It got more and more solid, a ghost in reverse, until there were two Angels in the room.

'Phew!' said Rory. 'It worked.'

Amy nudged him. 'I think I've spotted a flaw in our plan.'

Another image had begun to shimmer into life.

'The mirror's between them! The Doctor was worried about someone walking in front of it, he didn't think where the new Angel would go! The image of the first Angel's still in the mirror, it's going to keep making new ones! They need to be looking at each other.'

She was still speaking as Rory leapt onto the stage. He pushed the mirror out of the way. It fell to the floor and shattered.

'Seven years' bad luck,' said Amy.

Rory grinned. 'Oh, I don't think so.'

The new image had gone. Amy looked at the two solid Weeping Angels, now almost nose to nose. They would be looking at each other, frozen solid, for ever.

Rory looked at his wife. 'I think,' he said, 'that I'm going to keep on being very lucky indeed.'

Epilogue

Amy and Rory and the two old ladies left the Angels and went off to meet the Doctor.

The queue of magic acts had been cleared away from the theatre, but Trafalgar Square was crowded. People were gathered around the Fourth Plinth.

'Just in there,' Amy heard the Doctor say to a couple of men. 'Make sure they keep facing each other.'

'What's going on?' she asked as they joined him.

He smiled. 'Oh, I think I've found something to put on the Fourth Plinth. A statue of two angels facing each other. I call it *Monument to the Missing*. I just had to pop back a few weeks and call in some favours. By the way, while I was there I booked our theatre tickets. Oh yes, and something else.' He beckoned to Mrs Hooper. 'Amber, I've got someone who wants to see you.'

Mrs Hooper started hobbling over to the Doctor. Then she saw what he was talking about. She dropped her walking stick and ran like the teenager she'd been only hours before. 'Max! Oh, Max!'

The little tan and white Jack Russell leapt into her arms.

'Where did he come from?' asked Amy.

The Doctor tried and failed to look modest. 'Oh, well, I just found Max's vet record, put the code for his ID chip into the sonic and tracked him down. I swapped him for a wodge of cash, and here we are!'

'Nice one!' said Amy. 'By the way, any idea what happened to Sammy Star?'

'No,' said the Doctor. 'Which is very good. All he wanted was fame and fortune. I think if he became very famous or very rich in the past, I'd have heard of him. I haven't heard of him. So he didn't. That might be punishment enough.' He frowned. 'Well, maybe not quite enough. I'm just hoping that all the girls he tricked found good lives back in the past like Amber Reynolds did.'

Amy gave a big, tired sigh. 'Time to go?'

The Doctor nodded. 'The Angels will be safe here. Trafalgar Square. It's never empty and it's never dark. Even if something goes wrong, they'll always be observed.' He strode off. 'Come on, Ponds! Back to the TARDIS!'

Amy and Rory stood for a moment, watching the Angels being lifted into place.

'Mrs Hooper told me about losing Max,' said Rory after a minute. 'A stranger came to the door and bought him off her dad. That's what made her run away.'

Amy's eyes widened. 'The Doctor said he went back in time – oh no! He did it! He made her run away! Should we tell her? Should we tell *him*?'

'No,' said Rory. 'You heard what she said. She wouldn't change it. She had a dreadful life here, before she ran away. Back in the past, she met her Albert. Had her girls.' He bent down and kissed her. 'You can put up with anything, if it means you get to be with the people you love.'

In the middle of the square, Mrs Hooper and Mrs Collins started to dance. For a moment, Amy saw them as they had been, two lost teenage girls. Amber Reynolds and Kylie Duncan, dancing at the VE Day party in 1945. Max ran around the women's ankles, barking happily.

Holding hands, Amy and Rory walked off after the Doctor.

As they went, they heard the two old ladies' voices lifted in song.

'It may be an hour, it may be a week, it may be fifty years. But I know we will find loving hearts still entwined, on the day we meet again...'

Quick Reads 📖

Books in the Quick Reads series

Quick Reads 📖

Fall in love with reading

Quick Reads are brilliantly written short new books by bestselling authors and celebrities. Whether you're an avid reader who wants a quick fix or haven't picked up a book since school, sit back, relax and let Quick Reads inspire you.

We would like to thank all our funders:

We would also like to thank all our partners in the Quick Reads project for their help and support:

NIACE • unionlearn • National Book Tokens
The Reading Agency • National Literacy Trust
Welsh Books Council • Welsh Government
The Big Plus Scotland • DELNI • NALA

We want to get the country reading

Quick Reads, World Book Day and World Book Night are initiatives designed to encourage everyone in the UK and Ireland – whatever your age – to read more and discover the joy of books.

Quick Reads launches on **14 February 2012**
Find out how you can get involved at www.**quickreads**.org.uk

World Book Day is on **1 March 2012**
Find out how you can get involved at www.**worldbookday**.com

World Book Night is on **23 April 2012**
Find out how you can get involved at www.**worldbooknight**.org

Quick Reads

Doctor Who: I Am a Dalek
Gareth Roberts

BBC Books

Equipped with space suits, golf clubs and a flag, the Doctor and Rose are planning to live it up on the Moon, Apollo-mission style. But the TARDIS has other plans, landing them instead in a village on the south coast of England; a picture-postcard sort of place where nothing much happens... until now.

Archaeologists have dug up a Roman mosaic, dating from the year 70 AD. It shows scenes from ancient myths, bunches of grapes – and a Dalek. A few days later a young woman, rushing to get to work, is knocked over and killed by a bus. Then she comes back to life.

It's not long before all hell breaks loose, and the Doctor and Rose must use all their courage and cunning against an alien enemy – and a not-quite-alien accomplice – who are intent on destroying humanity.

Featuring the Doctor and Rose as played by David Tennant and Billie Piper in the hit series from BBC Television.

Quick Reads

Doctor Who: Made of Steel
Terrance Dicks

BBC Books

A deadly night attack on an army base. Vehicles are destroyed, soldiers killed. The attackers vanish as swiftly as they came, taking highly advanced equipment with them.

Metal figures attack a shopping mall. But why do they only want a new games console from an ordinary electronics shop? An obscure government ministry is blown up – but, in the wreckage, no trace is found of the secret, state-of-the-art decoding equipment.

When the TARDIS returns the Doctor and Martha to Earth from a distant galaxy, they try to piece together the mystery. But someone – or something – is waiting for them. An old enemy stalks the night, men no longer made of flesh...

Featuring the Doctor and Martha as played by David Tennant and Freema Agyeman in the hit series from BBC Television.

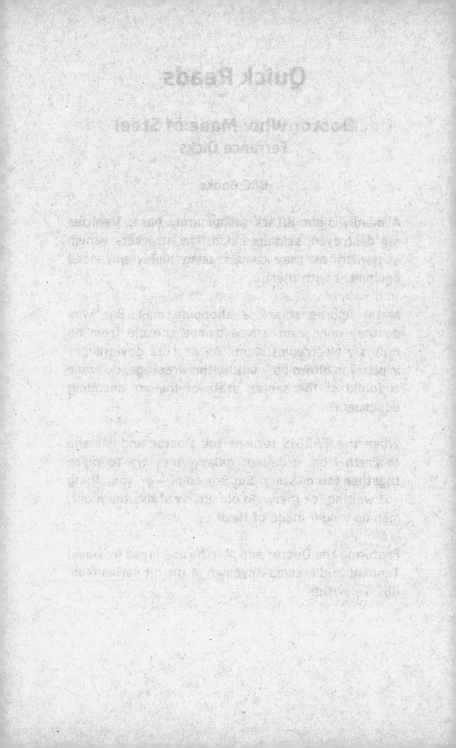

Quick Reads

Doctor Who: Revenge of the Judoon
Terrance Dicks

BBC Books

The TARDIS brings the Doctor and Martha to Balmoral in 1902. Here they meet Captain Harry Carruthers – friend of the new king, Edward VII. Together they head for the castle to see the king – only to find that Balmoral Castle has gone, leaving just a hole in the ground. The Doctor realises it is the work of the Judoon – a race of ruthless space police.

While Martha and Carruthers seek answers in London, the Doctor finds himself in what should be the most deserted place on Earth – and he is not alone.

Featuring the Doctor and Martha as played by David Tennant and Freema Agyeman in the hit series from BBC Television.

Quick Reads

Doctor Who: The Sontaran Games
Jacqueline Rayner

BBC Books

Every time the lights go out, someone dies...

The TARDIS lands at an academy for top athletes, all hoping to be chosen for the forthcoming Globe Games. But is one of them driven enough to resort to murder? The Doctor discovers that the students have been hushing up unexplained deaths.

Teaming up with a young swimmer called Emma, the Doctor begins to investigate – but he doesn't expect to find a squad of Sontarans invading the academy!

As the Sontarans begin their own lethal version of the Globe Games, the Doctor and Emma must find out what's really going on. But the Doctor is captured and forced to take part in the Sontaran Games. Can even a Time Lord survive this deadly contest?

Featuring the Doctor as played by David Tennant in the acclaimed hit series from BBC Television.

Quick Reads

Doctor Who: Code of the Krillitanes
Justin Richards

BBC Books

Can eating a bag of crisps really make you more clever? The company that makes the crisps says so, and they seem to be right.

But the Doctor is worried. Who would want to make people more brainy? And why?

With just his sonic screwdriver and a supermarket trolley full of crisps, the Doctor sets out to find the truth. The answer is scary – the Krillitanes are back on Earth, and everyone is at risk!

Last time they took over a school. This time they have hijacked the internet. Whatever they are up to, it's big and it's nasty.

Only the Doctor can stop them – if he isn't already too late...

Featuring the Doctor as played by David Tennant in the acclaimed hit series from BBC Television.

Other resources

Enjoy this book? Find out about all the others from
www.quickreads.org.uk

Free courses are available for anyone who wants to develop
their skills. You can attend the courses in your local area.
If you'd like to find out more, phone 0800 66 0800.

For more information on developing your skills in Scotland
visit www.**thebigplus**.com

Join the Reading Agency's Six Book Challenge at
www.**sixbookchallenge**.org.uk

Publishers Barrington Stoke and New Island
also provide books for new readers.
www.**barringtonstoke**.co.uk • www.**newisland**.ie

The BBC runs an adult basic skills campaign.
See www.**bbc**.co.uk/**skillswise**